Felicia's Nose[*]
by Carol Novack
(1948-2011)

*annotated by Tom Bradley

illustrations by Nick Patterson

MadHat Press
Asheville, North Carolina

MadHat Press
MadHat Incorporated
PO Box 8364, Asheville, NC 28814

The Library of Congress has assigned
this edition a Control Number of
2012952884

ISBN 978-0-9885490-0-5 (paperback)

Cover image: *Pseudo-Bibi porks "Hadrian" the gardener*
by Nick Patterson

Text by Carol Novack and Tom Bradley
Cover and interior illustrations by Nick Patterson
Book and cover design by Jonathan Penton

www.madhat-press.com

ANNOTATOR'S NOTE

At the end of her life, Carol Novack was doing what must eventually be done by everyone who's strong enough: she was squarely facing certain aspects of herself, her family, and her heritage that were not precisely excruciating, but, as she said, were "interesting and worthy of painstaking examination."

Even before the cancer diagnosis, she was tallying up her life's debits and credits, in particular the wheels and deals with *Muter*. The penultimate chapter of *Felicia's Nose* is a confrontation between the eponymous heroine and her female parent, ending with something like a Pandora's box being stashed under a bed. It's unopened, and bursting with what we all know is inside.

Being a writer, Carol's method of self-excavation was literary, and she recruited my help, two shovels being better than one. She liked the way I'd glossed Kane X. Faucher's sextuply schizoid impersonations in *Epigonesia* (BlazeVOX, 2010). That giant book fascinated Carol as the rarity of rarities: a new genre, something like a superficially nonfictional *Pale Fire*, taking place in real time as the primary text alternately rides roughshod over, and is sapped and subverted by, the critical apparatus.

She wanted me to do to her what I did to Kane X. Faucher in *Epigonesia*: to dig under her characters and situations, to dissect her names, numbers, references, to turn her allusions, both deliberate and unconscious, inside out. Carol wanted a running commentary that furtively pursued—she cringed at the word—*psychoanalytical* strategies. She envisaged an infestation of ten-point type skittering along the bottom of her novel like army ants underfoot.

"We need a literal *sub*text!" she cried.

The relationship of a novelist with her annotator is a bizarre admixture of banter and intimacy. As we worked, certain passages of her novel began to emit unexpected, sometimes appalling reverberations. But Carol never failed, with surprising courage, to reassure me that we were on track—or at least we were groping along an alley in a not-excessively dark and horrendous inner city.

Carol died before we could finish *Felicia's Nose*. In what neither of us knew would be her last chapter, she comes forward and speaks in her own voice for the first time. She shouts encouragement directly down to me, where I toil in cackling paranoia at the bottom of the final page. Carol's thinking about all the strange and possibly happy directions our book will follow next, and she says, "I can't wait to see…"

She didn't wait. I'll never know what she saw.

—Tom Bradley
tombradley.org

FELICIA'S NOSE

BY

CAROL NOVACK

FELICIA'S NOSE

Felicia de Rathbaum,[1] descended from a wayward line of
bellicose German, American, and Italian barons consumed by
a ravenous envy of lords, is at present sensually incarcerated

---

1   German-Jewish surname: *Rat* (German), "council": *Baum* (German),
   "tree." The Council Tree (*Ficus altissima*) produces inedible figs. Its
   Levantine cousin was cursed and sterilized by Christ, as follows:

   *Now in the morning as he returned into the city, he hungered. And
   when he saw a fig tree in the way, he came to it, and found nothing
   thereon, but leaves only, and said unto it, Let no fruit grow on thee
   henceforward for ever. And presently the fig tree withered away.*
   —Matthew 21:18-19

   The range of *Ficus altissima* (categorized by the USDA as an
   "invasive" species) is coextensive with the borders of Florida,
   elephant graveyard of numerous postmenopausal (withered and
   fruitless) bearers of the *Rathbaum* category of specification.

   In this esoteric context, the bare mention of any tree whatsoever
   suggests the Qabalistic Sephiroth, or, alternatively, the Tree of
   Knowledge, of whose morally inedible fruit Adam ate. *The Book
   of Reziel* depicts the latter apologizing to YHWH for said trespass,
   whereupon the eponymous angel, whose occult designation is
   Keeper of Secrets, appears in the quality of Councillor of the Tree of
   Knowledge, to instruct the First Man.

   Our (barren?) baroness begins by evoking her own esoteric alias,
   clearly claiming avatarship of that Promethean angel. She hereby
   presents us fallen first men with her *felicitous* book of accursed
   Rabbinical Wisdom—which, after these more-or-less pious
   preliminaries, will presently degenerate, or apotheosize, into a
   grimoire. (See note 28, on the notorious *Sefer Raziel HaMalakh*.)

Reziel, Councillor of the Tree

by the ghastly ashen scent of hoary black bear,[2] the beast

out of sight but threatening unconsciously the temporary

obliteration of consciousness, not to mention sub-. She

gasps, barely able to breathe. Into her royal, aquiline [3] nose

goes the cure: a bouquet garni of herbs and May flowers,

worn as a headcape.[4] Under a flow of succulent, satiny

---

2 The Chaldeans and the Egyptians (from whom Moses adopted the
   Cherubs in their animal form) symbolized Reziel's peers alchemically
   as follows: the Lion (Mikael); the Bull (Uriel); the Dragon (Raphael);
   the Eagle (Gabriel). The Bear was assigned to Thot-Sabaoth, who
   here, quite lawlessly, gives place to Reziel.

3 Special attention needs to be paid to the modifier *aquiline* as applied
   to our anti-Reziel's all-important nose. Gabriel's functionality may
   be similarly usurped in the pages to come. This insult to the astral
   hierarchy points out the left-path nature of the present volume.

4 The ancient Thaumaturgists made an especial study of the physical
   and moral reactivity of perfumes and incense. In their baneful
   conjurations they found it necessary to provide a material vehicle for
   the manifesting demon. Quantities of the appropriate incenses were
   burnt, so that from the haze of heavy particles a physical body could
   be constructed. Felicia's nose is the Jacob's ladder in an airborne
   Frankenstein operation.

   According to Israel Regardie, benzoin and sandalwood were used
   for Venusian spirits, mace and storax for Mercurial. Saturnians
   found sulphur congenial, while solar forces preferred galbanum and
   cinnamon.

   It remains to be seen—or, rather, *smelled*—in subsequent pages,
   to what nefarious purposes this tome's eponymous nose will be
   employed.

11

water filtered from the perpetual spring[5] of the delapidating[6]

estate of her fathers and mothers in memory, the prematurely

late Baron de Rathbaum X, the estranged *muter*[7] in the west

wing, *et cetera* (who settled on this mountain in Asheville,

---

5 See note 8, on the occult efficacy of "living" or spring water.

6 Deliberate heterography (in the pre-"linguistic" nineteenth-century sense) is but one of the hoary hand-sleights by which grimoirists can insinuate extra layers of perversity into their liturgies and recipe books. And, of course, far from betraying subliteracy, these seeming solecisms are invitations for alternative etymologizing, as follows:

To *de-lapidate*, presumably, is to perform the salvific service that Christ, in the eighth chapter of John's gospel, rendered unto the "woman taken in adultery," aka Magdalen: the Levantine Kali Avatar, the Tantric Initiatrix—and, of course, this transgressive text's presiding spirit.

Alternatively, *de-lapidation* could signify the retrieval of an entity from petrifaction, the reversal of the crone Medusa's chore. Or the apparent barbarism can be interpreted simply as the first categorical transformation in the Zoharic scheme: "First a stone, then a plant, then an animal, then a man, then an angel, then a god." Depending on the extent of their hubris, the baronial estate to which the de Rathbaums ascended would correspond to one of the upper rungs of this ladder.

7 Felicia will soon find herself simultaneously playing the roles of Electra and her estranged *muter* Clytemnestra. (See notes 26 and 78.)

North Carolina[8] in 1818[9]), felicia hies, disrobing to the

orgasmic orchestration of *Lieberstrom*, a rare recording by

Pesquanini. She immerses her copious, dream-pink corpus[10]

---

8   Asheville is the City of Ashes. Here the city can only be The
    City (Jerusalem), and it follows that the ashes must be those of a
    red heifer—i.e., the powdery prerequisites of the Third Temple's
    impending apocalyptic reconstruction.

    The Mishnaic tractate *Parah* in *Seder Taharot* sets out the procedures
    and recipe for the Red Heifer Ceremonial. The requisite moisture
    must be "living" water drawn from the Spring of Shiloah by a bizarre
    race of children, bred and reared as it were in hermetic isolation to
    prevent their incurring ritual taint through proximity or contact with
    corpses.

    In the pages to come, any juvenile manifestation will require the most
    exacting attention. The student of this transgressional genre known
    as grimoire can predict, even now, that the strange youngsters will
    appear juxtaposed with cadavers, or some other morally corrupting
    influence emblematic of spiritual death. (See note 42.)

9   "Baphomet" (aka The Sabbatic Goat—see notes 69, 72, 79 and 80)
    is first conjured in English on the pages of Henry Hallam's *The
    View of the State of Europe during the Middle Ages*, published in the
    significant year of 1818. Thus, in occult circles, this "brace of trebled
    sixes" carries the highest Gematrical value.

    In Asheville, a.k.a. Jerusalem, the Knights Templar unearthed a
    horned skull among the rubble to which the Romans had reduced
    Herod's splendiferous temple more than a millennium before. This
    fossil they venerated as the head of *Baphomet*, and performed
    analingual sacraments in its honor.

10 *copious, dream-pink corpus*: the baroness here assumes the floridly
    bovine attributes of the red heifer, pre-holocaust. Like any competent
    sorceress (and/or authoress), she offers herself up sacrificially.

with nose in the flow and ebb of the Wagnerian tsunami[11]

and forgets the host of unseen, odorous animals[12] that disrupt

the melodies of her senses. She invents yet another baron

of her own for her lumpy feather bed, reaches the high C

of her expansive imagination at the concept of his sublime

equanimity. Above all, Felicia desires . . . PEACE. She

needs the man of her desires,[13] or a reasonable facsimile,[14]

to rid herself of the need for him. Biological aches must

---

11 *Pesquanini ... Wagnerian tsunami*: with this symphonic recording,
    fancifully Italian, adjectivally German, metaphorically Japanese,
    Felicia saturates her eardrums in the Axis Powers, formerly so
    inimical to her people. She finds the sounds "orgasmic." This is an apt
    accompaniment to the book's sheerly perverse tenor.

12 These would be the disincarnate centers of inchoate consciousness
    that gather like moths around the glow of arcane workings—

    ... our Gnomes, our Undines, Salamanders, Sylphs,
    our Elementals and their mighty ilk.
    —Epigonesia, p. 186, note 169

13 *desires ... desires*: see note 28.

14 The modifier "reasonable" couldn't be more ironically intended
    in this quasi-alchemical context, with "facsimile's" intimations of
    the mud-engendered golem, the *fetiform teratoma*, the *fetus in fetu*,
    the homuncular embryo manufactured with messianic potential,
    molded of mischief, "asphaltick slyme," and other carbon-composed
    depravities—but deficient of spirit and soul as of pineal and pituitary.
    (See note 45.)

be quelled. Her trysts with Adrian the gardener[15] amount
to nothing more than postponements and there are more
pressing matters. The country is in a state of shell shock, its
residents paralyzed with fear and impotent rage.

It is well known by those who wish to know such trivia
that the bane of the baronesses of this line has always been
a sense of smell sufficiently acute to render its inheritors
comatose, whether it be hideous beyond description (words
are inadequate to delineate the experiences of the nose) or (as
in the mind's eye) extraterrestrially delicious, like a bouquet
of newborn (fill in your favorite flowers). The out-of-print
history books, though hardly dwelling on this minor noble
family, with its roots, as has been said, in the dungeons of
Pharaohs,[16] Third Millennium of The Age of Savage Inequity,

---

15 See note 1, pertaining to a different misdemeanor committed in
   another garden, by way of quelling biological aches.

16 If the baroness's surname is indeed Jewish, and if her line is of the
   antiquity here claimed, her ancestors will have been counted among
   the expelled lepers, idling day-laborers, streetwalkers *et al.*, from
   among whose ragtag ranks Moses improvised an ethnicity, complete
   with nonce language, in the Sinai. This is according to Ptolemaic
   priest Manetho, whose book the Jewish historian Josephus seems to
   have been the last person to peruse.

make reference to dubious reports that the barony was born from an uncommon callow fellow and his nursemaid, quarantined in the pits by certain querulous young scions of the omniscient royal families of the time. The Truth is not known; let us not succumb to myth and rumor,[17] as the hoards[18] are wont to do, worshiping their neighborhood gods and claiming the highest stake in the circle of celestial sanctuaries. Suffice it to say that the Present presents you, dear readers, with the protagonist Felicia de Rathbaum, who will be described principally by her actions and utterances, as opposed to an endless array of adjectives. Thus, Felicia is neither "kind," "good," "haughty," "hot," nor "pugnacious." Nor is she not. Like the rest of us, she is wending her way through the minefields of existence, too frequently with tight shoes that pinch her feet and will ultimately grow loose with

---

17 This is an overt plea, or an admonition to the present annotator, or perhaps a sop thrown to propitiate the mythopoeic tendencies that sometimes override his faithfulness to demonstrable fact. (See note 84.)

18 *hoards*: another example of left-path heterography, subliminally expressive of the tendency to see crowds not as masses of humanity, but as opportunities to amass profit, as in another Baron's famous maxim, "The time to invest is when blood runs in the street."

when blood runs in the street

age, like sagging body parts.[19] But the authors digress, as Felicia gets dressed.

And enters Priscilla[20] of the unpronounceable African[21] last
name, the essential companion to a woman of fast-dwindling
means,[22] with a dusty PhD in cetology. Felicia had written

---

20 Priscilla: one of the earliest Christian converts from Judaism, a
resident of Rome, possible author of the Book of Hebrews.

In her quality as pubescent Saint *Prisca*, she refused to obey an order
direct from Emperor Claudius to sacrifice to Apollo, so was beaten,
imprisoned, flogged, drenched in burning tallow, thrown to lions
(who purred at her feet), starved, stretched on the rack, torn with iron
hooks, thrust into a pile of burning wood, then beheaded because she
was tardy in joining her Merciful Father in heaven.

So high a pain threshold will come in handy for Felicia's live-in
companion. In the film version of this (see note 26), unhappy Saint
Prisca's nose will be struck by the owner of the present volume's
eponymous nose, and caused, more or less magically, to *bleed*—

*The potency inherent in blood, daubed and pooled with correct
ceremoniousness at each point of a Triangle of Art, can furnish
immaterial beings the stuff via which to make themselves manifest,*
—*Elmer Crowley* (Mandrake of Oxford)

(cf. Psedudo-Agrippa, Book IV: *Carcasses are not raised
without blood.*)

21   See note 51.

22   See note 26.

19

her thesis on the humpback whale.[23] The nearest ocean is

many hours away.[24]

Complaining of psychic and physical aches, Priscilla dusts

Felicia's porcupine Pappagano,[25] who rolls on his back to be

---

23 *Canst thou draw out leviathan with an hook? or his tongue with a
    cord which thou lettest down? Canst thou put an hook into his nose?
    or bore his jaw through with a thorn? ... Canst thou fill his skin with
    barbed irons? or his head with fish spears? ... Who can open the
    doors of his face? his teeth are terrible round about. His scales are his
    pride, shut up together as with a close seal. One is so near to another,
    that no air can come between them ... The flakes of his flesh are
    joined together: they are firm in themselves; they cannot be moved...
    He maketh the deep to boil like a pot: he maketh the sea like a pot
    of ointment. He maketh a path to shine after him; one would think
    the deep to be hoary. Upon earth there is not his like, who is made
    without fear. He beholdeth all high things: he is a king over all the
    children of pride.*
    —Job 41:1-34

24 Job lived in Uz, in the desertified neighborhood of the Dead Sea,
    whose saline solution hardly supports brine shrimp, let alone
    cetaceans. And yet his book provides the Bible's first description of
    Leviathan. In her scholarship as well as personal life, Felicia suffers
    the deprivations of Job.

25 Esoteric heterography for *Papageno*, the baritone personification of
    Error in *The Magic Flute*, who contemplates murdering himself but
    is dissuaded by friends. Suicide prevention in this gregarious form
    is called The Papageno Effect. In a perverse touch typical of the
    present text, such salvific mollification is assigned to the unpersonable
    porcupine.

    Auto-expungement, vulgarly known as *The Svennar toodle-doo,* bears
    directly on the remainder of this chapter, which recapitulates the work

tickled and teased.

There's something you should know," says Priscilla,

smiling painfully in order to suppress what she suspects is

inappropriate laughter.[26]

Silence.

"Well, what?"

---

of a former director of toothpaste commercials on Swedish television,
who went on to film the Mozart opera in question, and to *auteur* the
movie presently being paraphrased (or parodied—see next note.)

26 In a film that has been called "one of the [twentieth] century's
great works of art" (Hubert Cohen, *Ingmar Bergman: The Art of
Confession*, New York: Twayne, 1993, p. 215), the heroine, a stage
actress (portrayed by Liv Ullmann), is in the middle of a performance
of *Electra* (whether Sophocles' or Euripides' version isn't made
clear) when she is filled with the urge to *laugh inappropriately*. Her
professional scruples cause her to become mute on the spot, and
to remain so after the curtain is rung abashedly down. Soon she
requires the personal nursing attentions of an *essential companion*, a
Saint Prisca, to suffer on her behalf—in this case to proxy-suppress
inappropriate laughter.

The climactic image of this movie (used in all the promotional
posters) comprises the two women's faces blended together along
a vertical axis: Electra and Clytemnestra mutually subsumed if not
reconciled.

"It concerns Adrian[27] the gardener."

Felicia grows red. "And what of the gardener? You know I hate gossip."

---

27 *Adrian*: a form of the Latin *Hadrianus*, most notably Publius Aelius Traianus Hadrianus Augustus, Roman Emperor from 117 to 138.

Cassius Dio reports that, in putting down the Bar Kokhba revolt, Hadrian killed 580,000 Jews. He permitted burial of the dead only after a period of six days (*Yerushalmi Taanith*, 4), thus deliberately outraging the kosher legislation of the Jewish sages, which states that the soul is in turmoil until the body is correctly interred.

Hadrian burned the sacred scroll on the Temple Mount and renamed the province *Syria Palaestina* (after the Philistines, murderers of Samson, begetters of Goliath)—hence today's *Palestinians*. He caused a wall to be built around Jerusalem, and allowed no Jews to come near the city (Lamentations 5:2).

Utter chaos ensued (*Yerushalmi Peah*, 7), after which not a single olive tree remained standing in the entire province. Our transgressive baroness has named her gardener after this mass murderer of olives.

This busy yard man (who, we later learn, has been intimate not only with her, but with a goat named for the sin of *desire*) answers to the moniker of history's most spectacular persecutor of Felicia's people. Perhaps this is our book's most telling transgression: our heroine has employed and turned loose on her property a creature whose name is invariably followed, in the traditional Hebrew books, with the curse "may his bones be crushed."

"It concerns the gardener and a goat."[28]

Silence as Priscilla giggles.[29]

"I'm losing patience. *Which* goat?"

---

28 In the *Sefer Raziel HaMalakh*, Reziel coaxes the contrite Adam to
   embark on a tantric course of transgressive felony, as follows:

> *When pigs or goats have sexual intercourse,*
> *the males with the females are able to produce ...*
> *Desire to be dirty. Desire pleasures and seek pleasures*
> *from below the earth, until the ends of the opening edges ...*

That a specific beast known for malodorousness appears in a
document with an eponymous nose, is no coincidence.

29 In the critically gushed-upon film which inspired this exchange, the
   actress who plays the part analogous to Priscilla shares a nickname
   with Benjamin Netanyahu, Israel's ninth "shepherd"—and also the
   thirteenth, which arithmetically cancels out his earlier tenure and
   makes him, ever so significantly, the *twelfth*. (See note 49.)

The present "Bibi's" break into the acting profession came by means
of a television commercial for a Swedish toothpaste called "Bris"—
named after a style of genital mutilation performed amongst this
volume's pertinent folk. The particular variant evoked is *metzitzah
b'peh*, where the rabbi fellates blood from the hacked prepuce. The
practice has been implicated in the spreading of herpes, often fatal to
the infant, hence the perhaps ineffective introduction of toothpaste
(and, by extension, general oral hygiene) into the rite.

"Well, it's not like I want to tell you this, but . . . he did the nasty thing to that goat."[30]

"The *nasty thing*? What are you talking about?"

"Well, he was like crouching and the goat you call Desirée[31] was laying on the grass in back with her belly up and . . . his pants was down."[32]

"Was *lying* down, and *were* down, Priscilla. And he was either crouching or not crouching, not *like* crouching."

---

30 *A goat-headed prince bounds forward among them; he ascends the throne, turns, and assuming a stooping posture, presents to the assembly a human face, which everyone comes forward to salute and kiss, their black tapers in their hands. With a hoarse laugh he recovers an upright posture, and then distributes ... secret instructions, occult medicines and poisons to his faithful bondsmen.* –Eliphas Levi, *Dogme et Rituel de la Haute Magie*

This book being an evocation, in Act III, below, a satisfactory specimen of such a goat will bound forward and present to us his nether face. It remains to be seen what *secret instructions* he will distribute amongst us, his faithful bondsmen. (See note 64.)

31 See note 28.

32 Close to a verbatim reprise of an anecdotal confession of orgiastic sex delivered by Priscilla/Bibi in the film.

Clytemnestral Orgasm

"Oh, I'm so stupid and my tummy hurts and English makes no sense."

"I agree the language makes no sense,[33] and it's sounding ghastlier and ghastlier as the American version devolves, ear-piercing, actually, to anyone with sensitive ears, but you're not stupid and you don't eat properly. Oh, what's the use? I bore myself telling you this over and over again and you don't listen. I repeat: you can't eat Hostess Twinkies with milk for breakfast, lunch, and dinner, well maybe, okay, some chicken and rice for dinner every other day, and expect your digestive system to be happy. You're probably lactose-intolerant. As far as Adrian's concerned, the smell of goats doesn't thrill me. If he's been intimate with Desirée,[34] I'll know soon enough, but really, I don't care; I'll simply steer

---

33 Israel Regardie is eloquent and insistent on the hyperlexical efficacy of barbarous syllables of invocation, such as these gems from Dr. Dee's Enochian Keys:

> *Eca, zodocare, Iad, goho. Torzodu odo kikale qaa!*
> *Zodacare od zodameranu! Zodorje, lape zodiredo,*
> *Noco Mada, das Iadapiel! Ilas! hoatahe Iaida!*

34 cf. note 9 for the fragrant analingual services offered by the Knights Templar to propitiate their Sabbatic Goat.

clear. His love life is his own business. I think I'll make

myself a goat-cheese omelet,[35] but quickly. The meeting

starts at noon and I'm itchy[36] with curiosity."

---

35 This proposed menu item, including secretions from a "quadruped that chews the cud and also divides the hoof" (Leviticus xi. 3; Deuteronomy xiv. 6) does not constitute a violation of kosher legislation; but there is a deeper underlayer of transgression, flouting the autonomic gag reflex shared by Jew and Gentile alike. Significantly, in a book whose title includes a nose, and whose heroine's chief attribute is her superior olfaction, the recipe includes a proverbially miasmatic category of cheese.

36 *For the time will come when they will not endure sound doctrine; but after their own lusts shall they heap to themselves teachers, having itching ears.* (Emphasis added.)
—2 Timothy 4:3

The Heydays

During the *HeyheyHoHo Richard Nixon's Got to Go* daze of

the Vietnam War era, a certain materialistically well-endowed

Yippie so-called actor named Harry Smith-Harrington III

bought an abandoned Morman[37] church in Black Mountain[38]

for purposes of "disorganizing for the world's good." The

disorganization "Hold Hands for Humanity" (*HHH* [39]),

---

37 See note 6 with regard to orthographic transgression, and the implicit
demand for interpretation. Disregard the great-leveling "spell check"
and delve into the deeper significance of this ostensible mistake.

38 *This is the symbolic Mountain of God at the center of the Universe,
the sacred Rosicrucian Mountain of Initiation, the Mystic Mountain of
Abiegnus. Below and around it are* blackness *and silence.*
—Israel Regardie, *The Golden Dawn: a complete course in practical
ceremonial magic*

39 *In connection with this doctrine of the Tetragrammaton ... [the]
Father is given the letter "Y" of this name, and the first "H" is
attributed to the Mother. From the union of the Y and the H flow the
rest of all created things ... In the* Zohar, *the [final] letter "H" of
the divine name is called the Daughter, being the mundane reflection
of the first "H," which is the Mother. This tenth Sephirah is called
elsewhere the Bride, the Daughter, and the Virgin of the World.*
—Israel Regardie, *The Tree of Life*

initially a psycho-melodrama[40] group consisting of Harry's

five friends, his mother Gertrude,[41] and his occasional

paramour Willow, with their good-natured baby girl "Happy

Hence the triple repetition of the letter in the acronym, which also
calls to mind the Guadalupe Seer's threefold designation of the Virgin
of the World in another manifestation: *My Queen, my Lady, my Little
Girl.* Here they materialize as *Mother, Paramour* and *Baby.*

40 Overt admission that mysteries of the Eleusinian sort are afoot. See
note 48.

41 With this announcement that we are in the presence of *the son of
Gertrude*, yet another arcane female trio is conjured. Up in front
of our mind's eye spring and hobble the weird sisters who waylaid
and chatted up this son. Their own recipe for transgressing the
Darwinian gag reflex includes religio-ethnic, bestiarial and anatomical
ingredients which are already well stirred into the cauldron presently
boiling and bubbling before us—

> *Liver of blaspheming Jew;*
> *Gall of goat, and slips of yew*
> *Sliver'd in the moon's eclipse;*
> *Nose of Turk, and Tartar's lips;*
> *Finger of birth-strangled babe*
> *Ditch-deliver'd by a drab ...*

From note 29 springs the retroactively aborted infant (in this case
dispatched by human papilloma virus); the *delivering drab* is
none other than the crone of note 19; the *Turk's nose* needs only
undergo a particularly discouraged conversion, and perhaps gender
reassignment, to fit, plainly, up-front and center, on our title page.

Teeth,"[42] aka Karma,[43] met on alternate Thursday nights to plan the underthrow of "the Established Disorder" by means of outlandishly metaphorical public displays and ostentatious speeches in the manner of The Theater of the Absurd (think Ionesco[44]).

---

42 *There is a legend in which it is related of Christ Jesus that He, along with others, passed the dead body of a dog. The others turned away from the hideous sight, but Christ spoke admiringly of the creature's* happy teeth. (Emphasis added.)
—Rudolf Steiner, *Outline of Occult Science*

Here the very embodiment of human felicity, a good-natured infant, is invoked with the sort of necrophilic chaperone predicted above in note 8. It will be remarked that the present annotator, even in his mentally prepared condition, was unable to anticipate the special depth of morbidity achieved here: the corpse draped and drooling over the child, pedophile-priestlike, is not even human.

43 The force to which mere heredity plays handmaiden—see note 68.

44 A none-too-subtle signal that dramatic doings (as in initiatory mysteries) are afoot, in particular those of a quasi-Taoistically "indifferent" nature.

Felicia's Nose

Within seven weeks,[45] the disorganization numbered 38,[46]

---

45 The forty-ninth day of gestation enjoys a particular significance
in embryology lore, as related to the chore of Baubo, and the
metensomatotic miracle that requires the full obscene talents of this
headless gnomess as she diverts Demeter's spirit in the midst of her
nose-dive into the zygote. This is Madame Blavatsky's "profoundest
of mythos."

*This diminutive humpbacked sprite (*Baubo *is her name) reifies
nothing less than the hominid embryo, complete with the gill slits and
piggy tail by which ontogeny recapitulates phylogeny, all wadded
up and waiting to be ensouled. Miss Baubo's job is to distract the
misgivings of the peregrine spirit before its irrevocable fall into
matter, as it hesitates at the vestibule of the womb whose confines it's
fixing to occupy ...*

> *Upon the Corinthian isthmus*
> *squats Baubo, whose taste is abysmous.*
> *Her menses are barf,*
> *her nappy's a scarf,*
> *and her nipples exhibit strabismus.*
>
> *This trashy young tramp from the Troad,*
> *whose trench was transmogged to her throat,*
> *has labia majora*
> *that mumble pejora-*
> *tive verse in the Phrygian mode ...*
> —Elmer Crowley (Mandrake of Oxford)

It is the time of ripeness for ensoulment. The new carcass of
Homo sapiens achieves metempsychosomatic availability with
the appearance of pineal and pituitary at the end of its seven-
times-seventh day. Tibetans say this is the time required for one
soul to incarnate onto the next body. Forty-nine days is when sex
differentiation occurs. The "Established Disorder" is becoming more
and less so.

46 Here we recall the contingent of Manetho's societal offscourings who

including a charismatic newly minted Modern English Lit Honors grad by the name of Lancet Ovalaine, who assumed (by unanimous vote) the seat of Chair of Pubic Relations and Outreach. Every other Thursday, Lancet would occupy an immense, ornate Edwardian throne onstage, next to Harry, Gertrude, Willow, and Happy Teeth. Exceptionally gifted at offering ridiculous suggestions for advancing the cause (such as throwing hashish-smoke[47] bombs into local police stations), Lancet would toss his long golden curls violently to and fro across his refined, cleft-chinned face as he spoke with studied eloquence. The Chair thus sucked a burgeoning bevy of discontented underage hippie girls into the orbit of the misnomered "church." The girls sat on the eroded red carpet beneath the stage to gaze at the "rock star of the absurd" and squealed without restraint, particularly during intermissions,

---

returned to the wilderness, where they remained for *thirty-eight* years, and died, except Joshua and Caleb. (cf. Numbers 14:20-39)

47 The intoxicant properties are less important than the mass of the individual smoke particles. See note 4 with regard to the provision of vehicles for embodying astrals.

when Lancet strummed a loosely strung guitar and sang out-
of-tune Fugs and Beatles songs.[48]

Wikipoetika credits HHH with five incidents of hashish-
bomb attacks on public figures and aedifices, resulting in
16 arrests, five incidents of lyrical bear-and-mountain-
lion theatrical attempts in public forums, during which 28
members of HHH were detained for indecent exposure
and "incomprehensible radical boisterousness," and nine
incidents of "unauthorized, reckless flying" that involved
thefts of tourist helicopters "for the purpose of inciting
atheistic riots." On April Fool's Day, 58[49]

---

48 *We can rest assured that the hierophants, with generations of
experience, knew all the secrets of set and setting. I am sure that
there was music, probably both vocal and instrumental, not loud but
with authority, coming from hither and yon, now from the depths
of the earth, now from outside, now a mere whisper infiltrating the
ear, flitting from place to place unaccountably. The hierophants may
well have known the art of releasing into the air various perfumes in
succession, and they must have contrived the music for a crescendo
of expectation, until suddenly the inner chamber was flung open and
spirits of light entered the room ...*
—Wasson, Hofmann, Ruck, *The Road to Eleusis*

49 In the *Assumption of Moses*, Enoch is given "fifty-eight times," as
follows:

bare-breasted hippie girls who claimed to be members

---

1. And I saw till that in this manner thirty-five shepherds undertook the pasturing (of the sheep), and they severally completed their periods as did the first; and others received them into their hands, to pasture them for their period, each shepherd in his own period. 2. And after that I saw in my vision all the birds of heaven coming, the eagles, the vultures, the kites, the ravens; but the eagles led all the birds; and they began to devour those sheep, and to pick out their eyes and to devour their flesh. 3. And the sheep cried out because their flesh was being devoured by the birds, and as for me I looked and lamented in my sleep over that shepherd who pastured the sheep. 4. And I saw until those sheep were devoured by the dogs and eagles and kites, and they left neither flesh nor skin nor sinew remaining on them till only their bones stood there: and their bones too fell to the earth and the sheep became few. 5. And I saw until that twenty-three had undertaken the pasturing and completed in their several periods fifty-eight *times.*

According to Enoch's reckoning, twenty-three *goyische* kings lorded over Israel until the destruction of Jerusalem in 70 AD. Thirty-five kings came before, making *fifty-eight* the Enochian number of rulers over Ancient Israel.

Enoch prognosticates an even dozen further "shepherds," starting with Ben-Gurion, who initiated this penultimately kosher Kali-Yuga with a chilling prophecy of his own—

All continents will become unified in a world alliance, at whose disposal will be an international police force. All armies will be abolished, and there will be no more war. In Jerusalem, the United Nations (a truly United Nations) will build a shrine of the prophets to serve the federated union of all continents. This will be the seat of the Supreme Court of mankind, to settle all controversies among the federated continents, as prophesied by Isaiah.
–Look *Magazine*, January 16, 1962

Twelve plus fifty-eight makes seventy, the proverbial totality of Israel's "shepherds" who will be severely judged before the anticipated total overhaul of the world order. Thus, the conspicuous insistence on the number in our text is another assertion of our Kali-Yugic subtext.

35

of "The Church of The Holy Hands" were picked up for

"soliciting" motorcyclists on The Blue Ridge[50] Parkway.

They were released after a phone call from a Republican

congressperson. It wasn't clear what the errant girls were

soliciting. According to Sheriff Barney Fleck, "they wasn't

speaking any kind of intelligent-like English, just some kind

of weird African- or Asian[51]-sounding gibberish hogwash."[52]

---

50 If Asheville is internal code for the Holy City of the Monotheists,
    then the Blue Ridge, east of Asheville, signifies the Mount of Olives,
    a limestone ridge just east of the Old City of Jerusalem and separated
    from it by the Wadi Kidron. It was placed under the municipality of
    Greater Jerusalem following the Six-Day War of 1967.

    The "Blueness" of this ridge is derived from the color of the heavens
    into which Christ rises in the first chapter of the Acts of the Apostles.

51 Rather, African *and* Asian: the Hamito-Semitic nonce-lingo which
    Manetho (see note 16) has Moses contriving among the volcanoes
    of the Sinai. These *shiksas* have been taught phonetically to mouth
    the hexes of Qabalah, like Hare Krishna tarts uncomprehendingly
    yammering pidgin Sanskrit in airports, but in this case to somewhat
    greater astral effect.

    In Western (in some quarters aka. *Aryan*) Europe, the chromosome
    Haplogroup E1b1b1 is almost as rare as *heterochromia iridis*.
    However, molecular evolutionists inform us that it's common among
    the Berbers indigenous to Morocco, Algeria and Tunisia. This genetic
    configuration is also found in one-fifth of the Ashkenazim, and
    accounts for nearly a third of Sephardic Y-chromosomes, making it a
    major founding lineage of the Sons of Shem. (Genesis 9: 18-27)

52 See note 33 on the hyperlexical efficacy of barbarous syllables of
    invocation.

As this Southern region was and still remains constricted

by The Bible Belt, the parents and grandparents of the

Hippie girls who (inter alia) refused to attend their families'

churches, "swore real bad," and were caught smoking

banana skins in their bedroom closets, formed a "civic

association" called "Families for the Unification of Families"

(affectionately referred to as FUF, pronounced FUFF) to rein

in the wayward daughters (and a few latent homosexual sons,

on the hush-hush). Led by John Morgan Powers, Captain of

the Swannanoa Police Department's Brass Band,

his wife Shirley, a German Shepard[53] breeder[54] active in the

local branch of the NRA, and Shirley's widowed preacher

mother Margaret Thornton Price, the association gathered

---

53 *she-pard*: more Felician heterography. In Dante's infernal bestiary the leopardess embodies lust of the most ferocious sort. To the Weeping Prophet, something even more sinister is suggested—

> *... a leopard shall watch over their cities: every one that goeth out thence shall be torn in pieces: because their transgressions are many, and their backslidings are increased.*
> —Jeremiah 5:6

54 This is Lilith, the bestial one, with her characteristic familiar spirit, canine in nature—

> *Give not that which is holy unto the dogs,*
> *neither cast ye your pearls before swine,*
> *lest they trample them under their feet*
> *and turn again and rend you.*
> —Matthew 7:6

> *Bestial and shameless,*
> *from the hollow of the earth*
> *leap chthonian dogs*
> *who never show a true sign to a mortal.*
> —Chaldaean Oracles

momentum with alacrity and numbered 641[55] when FUF

stormed the church on a cheerful Thursday night in June,

1969 and captured the 97 attendees. As Willow noted to

Harry, on the way to the worn seat of Buncombe County jail,

it was "a bit peculiar that none of those silly girls happened

to be around, wasn't it, Harry?" And indeed, the girls

were all in their homes, knitting American flags . . . to the

surprised delight of the FUF, which prostrated itself to thank

Jesus "for the miraculous return of our daughters."[56]

Four years and six months after their sentencing by the

congressman's uncle, the Honorable Horace J. Minton IV,

Lancet and Harry, and a few other major players falsely

accused and convicted of nefarious acts of endangering the

welfare of the community, attempted treason, and engaging

in profane acts intended to "corrupt the virtues of minor

---

55 One of the diminishingly few integers that refuse to submit to any
creditable gematria. The choice can only have been made after
painstaking research, a perversely sublime expression of the text's
sedulous contrariness.

56 For the hermetic significance of the Daughter, see note 39.

children,"[57] emerged from the local penitentiary[58] and soon disappeared from the region. For several months, parole officers scoured The Blue Ridge Parkway in vain. Eventually, the penal authorities abandoned hope of re-capturing the un-Americans and focused their efforts on an influx of itinerant Mexican laborers.

Which brings us to the present, so to speak: Felicia's meeting in the twice-abandoned church resurrected from weeds and soil erosion by the elegant and erudite Che[59] Ola,[60] none other than the clandestine offspring of Lancet Olavaine.

---

57 See note 8 on the bizarre race of children.

58 This is a veiled initiation rite, a mystery, like the book of Job properly read and understood, depicting the emergence from darkness both physical and psychical.

59 Hebrew, *YHWH will add* (a son). In this case the son can be called a *prince* if Che, Sr., is considered to have been the "king" of whatever anarcho-syndicalist wrinkle of Stalinist theory he currently is accused of. Place a whole-head hircine mask on the royal shoulders, and the goat-headed prince prophesied in note 30 is handily arrived at, complete with fundament-licking entourage.

60 The Sanskrit term for leaf or strip from a leaf of the talipot palm, used by subcontinental thaumaturges for scrawling in menstrual blood their infernal liturgies and recipes.

red heifer ceremonial

Act III[61]

Che Ola, master of metaphors and occasional mind reader

with a Masters in Fine Arts and PhD in contemporary South

American poetry, absently tossed his long black curls[62] to

and fro over the startling face he'd acquired from his French-

American father and Peruvian mother, a descendent of the

Incas.[63] As he stood on the dais of the church,[64] enunciating

the mission of "ACT III" ("I" the pronoun[65]) with expressive

flourishes of tongue and hand, Che oozed the insistent

passion of aging youth, circumspect hope, justified rage,

---

61 This structural device borrowed from the theater is an explicit tipping of the authorial hand. Greek drama was an epiphenomenon of the Bacchic mysteries.

62 See note 74.

63 Human sacrificers par excellence, hence heroes immemorial to all left-path sorcerers.

64 The goat-headed prince bounds forward.

65 Triply egoistic intoning of the Ipsissimus' bounding first-person-singular pronoun, the ultimate bearding of Jehovah, the sublimely lethal expression of Luciferian hubris.

and above all, ACTION. Gone were the days of the Yippies

and Hippies. Long dead was the ineffectual, infantile SDS

(Students for a Democratic Society[66]). Che described ACT

III as "a mature movement to shake the malignancy out

of the dying body of America, a movement potent in its

awareness that each of us is faced with the dread of existence

and inevitable death without an afterlife,[67] coupled with the

knowledge that we must articulate our own choices, as no

god, fascist, or cult guru will do it for us, a movement that

reaches out to other movements to create one united front.

Welcome to the anti-church of existentialism, newcomers.

Are you ready to ACT?"

Che spread his arms wide as he spoke. It was only the third

meeting, but the audience numbered over 150, thanks to the

---

66 The disingenuousness of this acronym's explication is a given. Any
number of truer interpretations are readily available, even to the
uninitiate mind.

67 An example of boilerplate fear-mongering to paralyze the uninitiate,
to render the outer-porch brethren hypersuggestible; a rudimentary
example of the ruse which the Brahmans perfected in *Manu's Code*.

PR campaign headed by Dorothea (the erstwhile Karma[68]), who was dextrous with the Internet, with more than 10,000 friends and fans on Facebook and an impressive number on Twitter.

A large portion of those present were massage therapists, yoga teachers and assorted New Agers. They considered themselves "spiritual;" while they were uncomfortable with Che's atheism, they were drawn to his intense and inspiring energy, and of course, they were interested in improving the lot of humanity. The belief in some god or amorphous concept of "spirituality" was a challenge Che would have to meet; it would be an uphill battle to convince these students of the pop "think positive" school that they would have to confront head-on the ugliness of "this" world in order to make their brief lives meaningful and fulfilling. Dwelling

---

68 Karma, the force that runs the universe, is among the few substantives to which the modifier "erstwhile" can never be attached.

It is, moreover, unquestionable that in case of human incarnations the law of Karma, racial or individual, overrides the subordinate tendencies of Heredity, its servant.
—Madame Blavatsky, *The Secret Doctrine*

on "the (false) positive" and the belief in a meaning imposed by something outside of themselves was ideologically inimical to the progress of the human species; indeed, belief was insidious oppression. Freedom could only be achieved through the realization of dread, the recognition of one's innate I-ness and the higher moral imperative that flowed from within. Che wanted to move the oppressed masses to believe in their own power, but he knew that he could hardly achieve this by himself, if at all. The Contras in Nicaragua had wrested away his father's power by means of violent indoctrination. As a child, Che witnessed the disintegration of his revered parent with horror. In the space of a decade, he aged from nine to 40. He would never be enslaved . . . nor would he enslave. He comprehended his own power.[69]

---

69 This entire paragraph serves the same function as the barbarous nonsense syllables: of no particular import, rather sounds that by their very lack of significance draw spirits of nihilism and decay. The first third of the paragraph constitutes a precis of the *secret instructions* distributed by Baphomet to his *faithful bondsmen*, as predicted above in note 30; the final two-thirds, in which the omniscient narrator feigns to penetrate the goat-headed prince's mind for a modicum of ostensible self-reflection, is more of the same, packaged for receipt by those members of the assembly who abide off the page and run their eyes across it.

Both sets of secret instructions are, of course, meaningless, as all such communications are in the essentially Taoist dialectic that

Felicia sat in the third row, trying to take notes. A few

pews back, someone was wearing "Shalimar,"[70] a perfume

---

prevails over left-path thaumaturgical workings. While not couched in barbarous phonemes, their dealing in the most superficial pseudo-philosophical quibbles renders them as ephemeral and sterile of intellectual challenge as the *Eca, zodocare, Iad, goho,* etc., of note 33, whose only function is to drone the weak mind to a condition of idle suggestibility.

After nonsense syllables, the most effective stupor-inducer available to the human vocal apparatus is the platitude, delivered in such nasal drone as can be imagined bleating from this goat's muzzle.

The only function being served here is the preparation and distribution of the hashish bombs, and even they have no point beyond their evocative properties. This is Taoistic blather for blather's sake.

The method therefore of acquiring (the word is to be preferred to "attaining") Indifference is simple; it is, in effect, the Way of the Tao... Existence is only to be understood as a Continuum. All parts of Existence are therefore ultimately equivalent, each being equally necessary to complete the whole. Each event is thus to be received with equal honour, and the reaction to it made with equal indifference.
—Aleister Crowley, *Little Essays Toward Truth*

70 A garden built by Praversena II, who founded the city of Srinagar and ruled in Kashmir from 79 AD to 139 AD. Early in his reign the Kushan emperor Kanishka convened the fourth Buddhist council in the neighborhood, which was responsible for translating texts that would serve as foundations for the Greater Vehicle school. It's likely the lovely Shalimar garden, after which our "nauseous" perfume is named, played host to lavish parties featuring Kanishka. This adds a suggestively Buddhist dimension to the utterance of the *woman on the left* (sinister sister), "Lord, he's divine. Just look at those eyes, and that bod."

that made her nauseous,[71] and the woman to the left was

whispering loudly and repeatedly to her female friend, in

various permutations: "Lord, he's divine. Just look at those

eyes, and that bod, Katie. I could just swoon.[72] Couldn't you?

I think if he told me to walk across a minefield, I'd do it.

Ohmygodohmygod!"[73]

After a question-and-answer period, Che asked the attendees

to sign up for various task groups. Lawyers were asked to

volunteer their services in kind to file documents to make

ACT III a non-profit organization; web designers, artists,

and developers were asked to create a logo and website.

---

71 *nauseous*: another of our baroness' deliberate barbarisms, not
   heterographical in this case, but a bathetic dip into substandard usage.
   In describing herself as evoking rather than suffering nausea, Felicia
   evinces the proverbial self-hate of the *meydl* who has lain with the
   most egregious gentile of all, *may his bones be crushed* (see note 27).

   She will soon allow herself to be ridden like a mule by another enemy
   of Israel and its temple: a more ineffectual foe than Hadrian, yet more
   intimately hurtful, being the brother of that temple's builder. (See note
   76.)

72 Standard systemic reaction in a kisser of the Baphometic fundament.

73 Another string of *barbarous syllables*, as mentioned above.

Marketing and PR professionals and others signed up to draft press releases and establish media contacts. People volunteered to organize rallies and meet with politicians; those with connections to the wealthy agreed to seek sponsors, a couple of grant writers signed up, and a few savvy activists, involved with other groups, signed up for outreach with other compatible non-profit organizations. And so it went. Attendees who chose to commit themselves lined up at the long table in back, where Karma and a few early recruits provided information and sign up sheets.

Felicia was hesitant to jump into this so-called movement, having a deep-seated distrust of groups and charismatic leaders. She would need to know more about Che and what he really intended to achieve. She would return. As Felicia was leaving, Che approached and fastened his eyes on hers.

"Please, whoever you are, I think you are hesitant about this organization and suspicious of me, with good reason;

there are so many false leaders about. But . . . I can recall
the dream you had last Tuesday, Shall I tell you what I
remember?"

Felicia almost stammered,[74] "I'm Felicia de Rathbaum. Mr.
Ola, I don't know whether you're offering more than sleights
of mind, which is troubling, considering, but if you must,
curiosity trumps suspicion." (*And I like the way you smell,*
she didn't say.)

"Forgive me, Felicia de Ratboom" Che responded.
"For some reason, that has nothing to do with mystical
explanations, I can sometimes recall other people's dreams
in which I've played a part. I see that last Sunday, you
dreamed of a mountain falling into a river. You were living

---

74 Absalom (see note 76) was the handsomest man in the realm, with
famously beautiful *long black curls* that proved his undoing. Small
wonder our otherwise-imperious baroness is rendered bashful and
artless as pubescent Saint Prisca smirking back inappropriate giggles.

Melding the nubile with the crone, the daughter with the mother: such
is the very theme of the cinematic version of all this (see note 26), and
of Felicia's own Electral complex. In the following chapter, *Muter*,
she will be demoted to the status of offspring, with the advent of her
Clytemnestra.

Felicia almost stammered, "I'm Felicia de Rathbaum."

on this mountain, as was I. We were carried away by the torrent of the water, moved by the powerful rains that stir the earth in this region. I tried to catch you as you rushed by, but you didn't look at me. You continued to struggle against the waves and I tried to save you. I said: Go with the waves and you will land on quiet land. But you refused to listen, kept on going. That is all. You disappeared as I clung to an oak tree,[75] and I awoke in a sweat. While I don't believe in

---

75 *And they gave unto Jacob all the* strange gods *which were in their hand, and all their earrings which were in their ears; and Jacob hid them under the oak which was by Shechem.*
—Genesis 35:4 (Emphasis added—see following note.)

premonitions, this dream has held me hostage.[76] Of course,

I didn't know who you were, and I don't know who you are

now . . .."

---

76 *And Absalom rode upon a mule, and the mule went under the thick
boughs of a great oak, and his head caught hold of the oak, and he
was taken up between the heaven and the earth; and the mule that
was under him went away.*
—2 Samuel 18:9

More bestiality in this increasingly zoophilic grimoire. We've merged
with the red heifer (note 10), fornicated with the Goat of Mendes
(note 71) and fraternized with Lilith, "the hairy one" and her pack
of Chthonian dogs, *bestial and shameless* (note 54). Now the barn
door is kicked open yet again to turn loose another theriomorph. It's
the *strange god* whose Solomonic temple worship is reported by
Posidonius and Apollonius, and whose head Antiochus discovered
on the premises, like the skull of Baphomet, when he despoiled the
sanctuary. (Josephus, *Contra Apionem*.)

Felicia is the mule: like Baphomet, a hermaphrodite-hybrid, the
product of licentious behavior analogous to bestiality in both the
equine and asinine tribes. Che-Absolom was "riding upon her" when
she left him hanging, "held hostage" by the dream-oak.

"I don't remember that dream, Mr. Ola, but my last name is Rathbaum, as in angry tree,[77] and I do live on a mountain. Of course, many of us here live on mountains. And I've probably had nightmares about drowning. We all do. Life is overwhelming, death is always around the corner, and too many people watch Fox News. People hate the president because he's black, and call him a Communist. Such a sick joke! So many stupid people in the position of drawing the ignorant into their idiotic circles. What's your point?"

"Not everything has to have a point, Ms. Rathbaum . . . Felicia, please call me Che. I agree with everything you say about this society. And I don't blame you for thinking me ridiculous and manipulative."

---

77 Like a teenaged neophyte to flirtation, she feigns toughness, and calls her name wrathful, trying, through more of her habitual heterography, to make the fig tree formidable as the oak.

This patent act of misanthroponymy is a blind, or veil, deliberately cast over the eyes of the uninitiate and vulgar by lending a reassuring affect of righteous indignation, as opposed to the sublimely inhuman quasi-Taoist *indifference* discussed in note 69. An even higher form of the Taoist affect is the *disinterest* of the *councillor*. See note 1 for the correct signification of our baroness' surname.

Felicia met Che's eyes. She saw the same earnest, painful urgency she'd heard in his voice, as he was speaking to all those present. For a few surprising seconds, she believed in his authenticity and for once, did not feel completely alone.

"I'll return, Che," she said, trying to imagine trust.

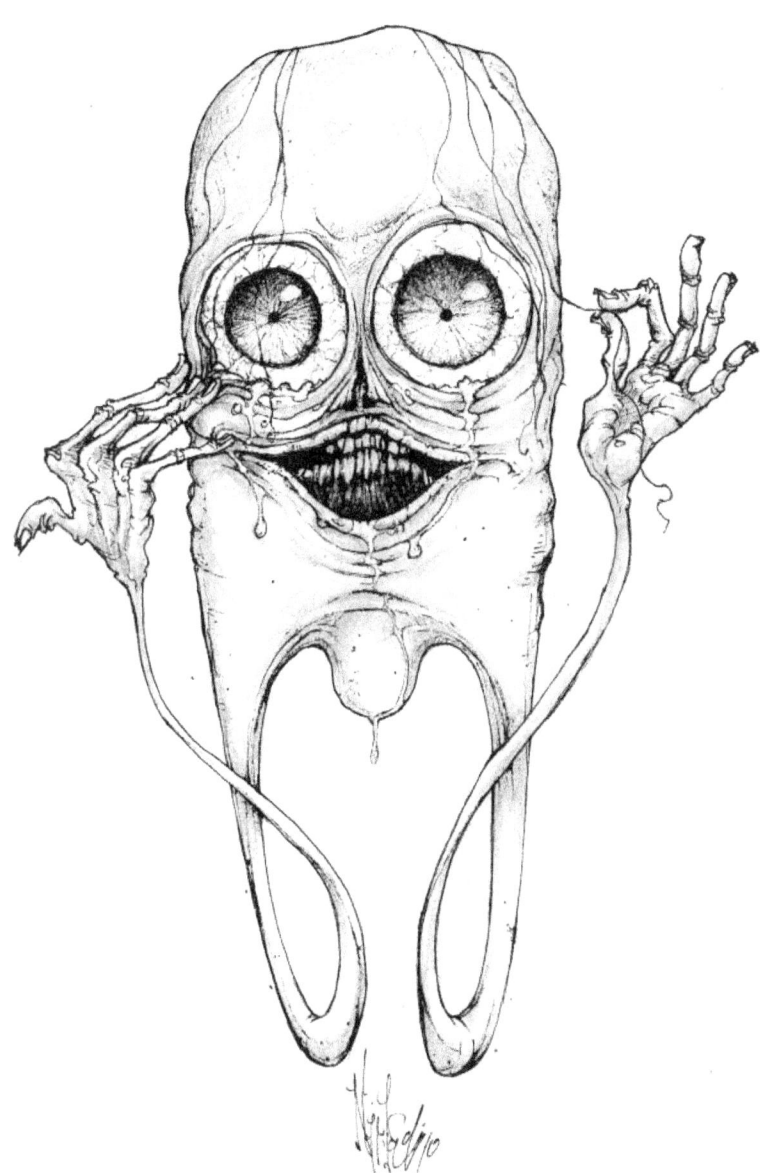

Hope…prolongs man's torment.

Muter[78]

Felicia's hermetic mother Lola[79] stood beside her daughter's
bed for a few moments, watching Felicia's eyelids tremble
with dreams. When Felicia moaned and cried, her mother
shook her out of sleep and screamed: "Stop that!"

Felicia sat up, abruptly: "Stop what?"

---

78 We are about to meet our Electra's horrendous Clytemnestra, the
object of her vengeful passion. Soon one or the other will be disposed
of, shunted out of sight, in a box.

79 Aleister Crowley (aka Baphomet, the epithet of the abovementioned
goat) so named his eldest daughter, followed by the barbarous syllable
Zaza in place of a middle name, as follows:

> *Sazaz Sazaz Adnatsan SazaZ (Pronounce this backwards.*
> *But it is very dangerous. It opens the Gates of Hell.*
> —*Liber Pyramidos* (commentary by Frater T.S.)

"You were having a disturbing dream. Such dreams dry your skin and take years from your life.[80] You had them frequently when you were a child."

"So all of a sudden, you care about my dreams?"

"I've always worried about your dreams, Felicia."

"Well, you never said anything."

"We took you to a child psychologist when you were five. I gather you don't remember. Typical." She sighs.

"No, I don't, and I don't believe you, mother dear. Truth has never been important to you."

"I didn't wake you up in order to be abused. I came to give you something, which you should keep in the bank safe-

---

80 Another crone transformation, as per note 19, above; the Goat of Mendes, aka Baphomet, is traditionally depicted as a hermaphrodite with grandmotherly dugs puckering and pendulating from its thorax.

deposit box. I've kept it hidden since your father died.
Now it is time to pass it to you. I won't survive the winter,
or summer, or whatever season this is. You won't see me
again."

"What are you talking about? You've always been so
melodramatic."[81]

"I've decided that my life is meaningless and boring, and
don't tell me I can do this or that to change my perspective.
There's no point in going on."

"Obviously, you're depressed. You chose years ago to
inhabit your own space, all alone, to let no one, even me, into
it. You emptied yourself of your self when Father died. I
remember clearly that you refused every possible therapeutic
treatment I suggested, so I gave up and let you alone, though
I needed you."

---

81 In the original Greek sense of a mystery rite with song, invocations.

"Your memory is not to be trusted, Felicia, but I'm not here to debate the past."

"Good. Don't. I have no interest in the past. But you're my mother, so I'll try to save you. An impulse I just can't resist. Guilt is the only social adhesive we have, pathetic species."

"Don't waste your time and energy, sweetheart. You're right, I am empty. I wish we were all ecstatic and simple, but we're not. Your hair's a mess, and that handmaiden of yours isn't doing a good job of keeping your apartment neat and clean. I hope you don't overpay her. There's not much left, as you no doubt know."

Lola retrieved the small, plain cardboard box she'd left by the door, and put it in her daughter's hands. She kissed Felicia on both cheeks, in the European style. "I've loved you as much as I could. It was never enough, but then, mother love

never is. Fire the gardener."[82] Then she departed, closing the
door after her.

Felicia took the box[83] and pushed it under her bed.

---

82 Perhaps a motherly euphemism for "crush his bones." (See note 27.)

83 *box*: like Felicia's many heterographies, a deliberate solecism.
Erasmus of Rotterdam, in translating Hesiod, botched *pithos* (jar) as
the Greek *pyxis* (box).

*Pandora brought the jar with the evils and opened it ... Then all the
evils, those winged beings, flew out of it ... One single evil had not yet
slipped out of the jar ... it is hope, for Zeus did not want man to throw
his life away, no matter how much the other evils might torment him,
but rather to go on letting himself be tormented anew. To that end, he
gives man hope. In truth, it is the most evil of evils because it prolongs
man's torment.*
—Nietzsche, *Human, All Too Human*

Felicia's mother, her hope and torment, is pushed under the bed,
where infantile monsters hibernate.

Carol Novack, Tom Bradley, Nick Patterson

The High Reverends

(Tom[84]: this page will be blank as far as the narrative is concerned. I encourage you to compose footnotes. Can't wait to see what you come up with!)

---

84 *The country gives me proof and precedent*
 Of Bedlam beggars, who, with roaring voices,
 Strike in their numb'd and mortified bare arms
 Pins, wooden pricks, nails, sprigs of rosemary;
 And with this horrible object, from low farms,
 Poor pelting villages, sheep-cotes, and mills,
 Sometime with lunatic bans, sometime with prayers,
 Enforce their charity ... poor Tom!
 —King Lear II.iii.13-19

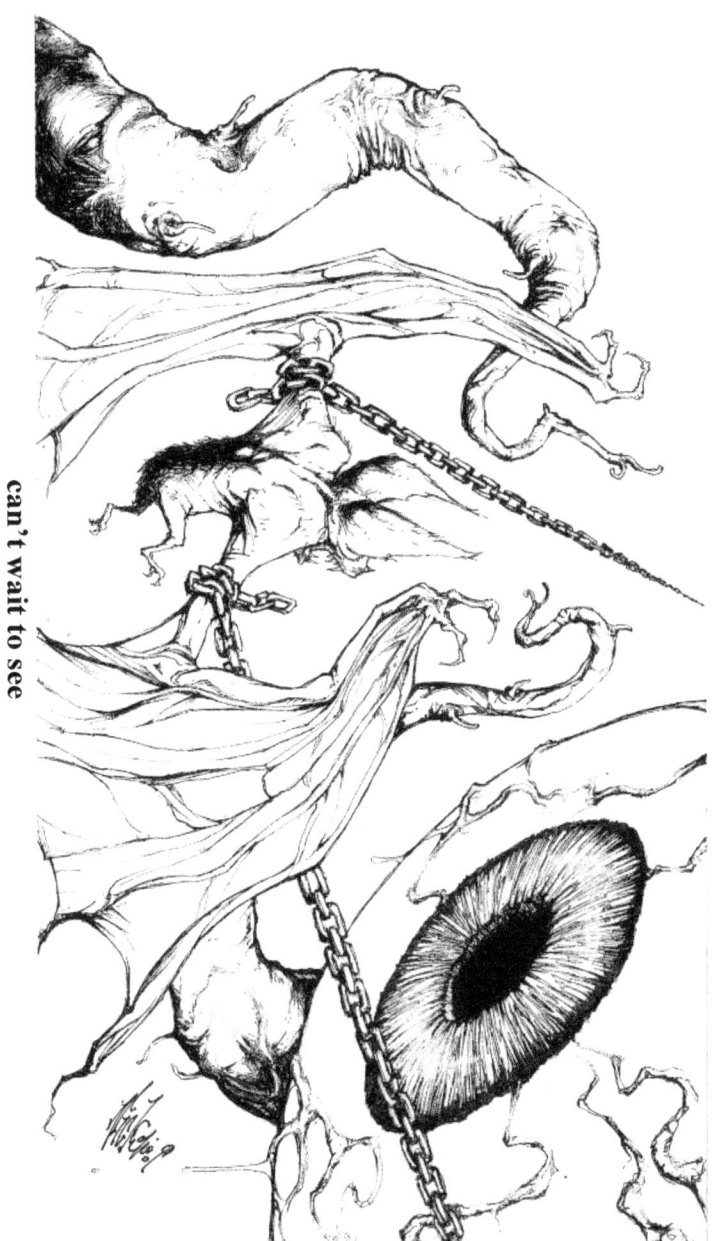

can't wait to see

Carol Novack, Tom Bradley, Nick Patterson

CAROL NOVACK (1948 - 2011) founded *Mad Hatters'
Review* in 2005, was the former recipient of a writer's
award from the Australian government, the author of a
poetry chapbook, and an erstwhile criminal defense and
constitutional lawyer in New York City. In 2010, she moved
from a Greenwich Village co-op to a mountain residence (a
future "retreat" for individuals and collaborators) in Western
North Carolina, importing her KGB Bar reading series,
"Poetry, Prose, and Anything Goes" to The Black Mountain
College Museum and Art Center, and founding the non-profit
arts organization, MadHat, Inc.

Carol's collection of fictions, fusions, monologues and poems,
Giraffes in Hiding: The Mythical Memoirs of Carol Novack,
was published in 2010 by Spuyten Duyvil Press. The book
is beautifully illustrated, mainly by artists who've graced the
pages of *Mad Hatters' Review*. The late poet Hugh Fox called
the collection: "The most seductive, original, impacting work
I have seen for years... Magnifique!"

TOM BRADLEY's latest books are *Family Romance* (Jaded
Ibis Press, illustrated by Nick Patterson), *A Pleasure Jaunt
With One of the Sex Workers Who Don't Exist in the People's
Republic of China* (Neopoiesis Press), *Even the Dog Won't
Touch Me* (Ahadada Press), *Hemorrhaging Slave of an Obese
Eunuch* (Dog Horn Publishing) and *Put It Down in a Book*
(Drill Press, *3:AM Magazine*'s Non-Fiction Book of the Year
2009). His next novel, with secret title and hidden nature,
illustrated by the alchemical artist David Aronson, is coming
next year from the occult publisher, Mandrake of Oxford.
Further curiosity can be indulged at tombradley.org.

NICK PATTERSON is a visual artist whose love of twisting minds and turning heads has led him to explore all the darkness the human experience can muster, through high contrast ink drawings. With no official training in the visual medium, Patterson's art is loosely tethered to reality, although it is very detailed. His inspiration is drawn from an amalgam of cartoons, comics, and movies. Carrying a sketchbook with him everywhere, he lets no flicker of imagination escape. Nick Patterson's art has been published in several small magazines and novels. He currently lives in a city full of flowers on the western edge of Canada.

www.ingramcontent.com/pod-product-compliance
Lightning Source LLC
Chambersburg PA
CBHW060135260626
47160CB00005B/2116